For Chip and a new generation, with love. —B. L.
For Roger Etnyre, with love. —B. M. J.

◀▶| ◀||▶ |◀▷| ◀▷| ◀|▶ |◀▷| ◀▷| ◀||▶ |◀▷

*The publisher gratefully acknowledges Dorothy Hodgson, Associate Professor
of Anthropology at Rutgers University, for her gracious guidance and
impeccable advice, which we took wherever we were able. Her suggestions
have helped to make this a better book.*

Book design by Mary Beth Fiorentino.
Typeset in Goudy.
The illustrations in this book were rendered in watercolor.
Manufactured by Great Wall Printing, Hong Kong, China in July 2010.

Library of Congress Cataloging-in-Publication Data
Joosse, Barbara M.
Papa, do you love me?/by Barbara Joosse; illustrated by Barbara Lavallee.
p. cm.

To host an author event with the author or illustrator of this book,
please contact: publicity@chroniclebooks.com.
Summary: When a Maasai father in Africa answers his son's questions, the
boy learns that his father's love for him is unconditional.
ISBN-10: 0-8118-4265-7
ISBN-13: 978-0-8118-4265-5
[1. Fathers and sons–Fiction. 2. Love–Fiction. 3. Maasai (African people)–Fiction.
4. Blacks–Africa–Fiction. 5. Africa–Fiction.] I.
Lavallee, Barbara, ill. II. Title.
PZ7.J7435Pap 2004
[E]–dc22
2003017344

10 9 8 7

This product conforms to CPSIA 2008.

Chronicle Books LLC
680 Second Street, San Francisco, California 94107

www.chroniclekids.com

Papa, Do You Love Me?

by Barbara M. Joosse   illustrated by Barbara Lavallee

chronicle books · san francisco

Papa, do you love me?

You came from your mama, whom I love,
your grandpapas and grandmamas, whom
I honor, and from me.

You are my Tender Heart, and I love you.

How much?

I love you more than
the warrior loves to leap,
more than the bush baby
loves the moon,
more than the elder
loves his stories.

How long?

I'll love you as long as the wildebeest run
on the mara, the hippopotamus wallows in
mud, and the Serenget rolls to the sky.

Papa, what would you do if I was hot?

We'd rest under a Greenheart tree.

What if the sun scorched the leaves
and they dropped off the branches?

Then I'd stretch out my blanket
till you were cool in my shade.

What if I was thirsty?

You would drink water from the calabash.

What if the calabash was dry?

You'd fill it from the river.

What if the river was dusty and the creek was cracked?

I'd teach you to look for hidden
streams and push through dry
earth until you reached water.

Then, Tender Heart, we'd
splash sweet water over
our tongues.

Papa, what if
I was the herd boy?

I would be proud.

What if I was the herd boy, and I ate roasted
meat till my belly was round, and I tried
to stay awake, and I tried to guard the cattle,
but my eyelids got drowsy?

Then I'd show you how to stay awake.
Together we'd sing to the full white moon
and dance to the sweep of stars until your
eyes were bright.

What if I fell asleep anyway and hyenas crept in
       and killed a cow . . . and it was my birthright cow?

Then, Tender Heart, I would be
angry. But still, I would love you.

What if I was afraid?

       I'd wrap my arms around you so you could hear
       my heart beat like a drum.

What if hyenas blinked yellow eyes at me?

       We'd throw back our heads and
          how-how-*hooowwwwwl*
       till they slank-slunk away.

What if a lion prowled in our camp, swished his tail, and rumbled for food . . . and *I* was his food?

Then, Tender Heart, I'd shelter you with my shield. I'd shake my spear at the beast till his great mane trembled and he cowered in his den.

I'll care for you, love you, and teach you.
Always.

Because I am your papa, and you are my
Tender Heart.

Glossary

BIRTHRIGHT ANIMALS A cow, a ewe, and a female goat are given to a Maasai boy when he is young. These animals, called *ingishu emisigiyoyi* (pronounced in-kee-shoo e-mis-ig-ee-yo-yi), are particularly significant, because they are the start of his herd.

CALABASH A calabash is a container made by Maasai women from a gourd and used to store liquid, such as milk or water or cow's blood.

CATTLE Cattle and children are a Maasai father's greatest treasures. When two Maasai meet, they  exchange the greeting, *"Keserian ingera? Keserian ingishu?"* (Kay-sear-ee-yan in-care-a? Kay-sear-ee-yan in-kee-shoo?) Which means, "How are the children? How are the cattle?"

DANCE Maasai men often take part in jumping dances. One or two stand in the center of a circle and try to jump the highest.

ELDERS It is the responsibility of the male elders to teach Maasai boys how to care for cattle, track animals, watch for enemies, and protect their families. They often teach by telling stories, especially at night around hearth fires.

ENKANG This is the word used to describe a Maasai settlement. Traditionally, Maasai women build igloo-shaped houses out of mud and cow dung, the two materials that are easiest to find. The houses are surrounded by a circular, prickly fence. At night, cattle are driven into the center of the *enkang* to protect them from predators.

GREENHEART TREE (or Pepper Bark Tree) This tree stands tall and solitary on the Serengeti, looking very much like a Maasai herdsman. The tree's bark is used to heal stomachaches, fevers, toothaches, and muscle pain.

HERD BOY The herd boy holds a position of great responsibility. It is his job to keep the cattle safe during the daytime. It would be unlikely for a father and son to watch over a herd at night without the protection of warriors. This part of the story represents the boy's worries that he would fail at such an important job.

MARA The Maasai mara is in Kenya and is part of the Serengeti Plain.

RESPECT A Maasai boy shows respect, *enkanyit* (en-can-yit), by serving and working for his parents.

ROBES Some Maasai wear a red robe patterned after the wool blankets brought to Kenya by the British. They also decorate their bodies with colorful beaded jewelry and sometimes red ocher and white chalk.

SERENGET (or Serengeti) This is another name for large parts of Maasailand, an area that covers parts of Kenya and Tanzania. It supports the highest concentration of wildlife on the earth.

SHIELD When a warrior kills a buffalo he takes the hide to his camp to make a shield. He decorates the shield with paint to record his bravery.

SPEAR A spear is a Maasai warrior's most precious possession. He polishes the tip with animal fat each day.

TENDER HEART Like fathers everywhere, Maasai fathers call their sons special names. They often reflect a connection to their ancestors.

WARRIOR To become a warrior, a young, unmarried man goes through a ritual that tests his strength, endurance, and bravery.

WATER is very precious on the mara. Women strap heavy jugs to their heads or to the backs of donkeys and walk a long, long way to bring water to their families. The Maasai must be very clever to coax water from dry creek beds and find hidden springs.